The Atlantic Wall in France 1940-1944

Luc Braeuer

Acknowledgements

We address our thanks to all those who have loaned documents and helped us with the realisation of this volume, in particular: Marc Braeuer, Alain Chazette, Laurent Cochet, Alain Destouches, Alain Durrieu, Michel van Heuwermeiren, Sébastien Hervouet, Jean Michel, Rodolphe Naegele, Michael Schmeelke.

Luc Braeuer

Photo credits: Luc Braeuer, unless otherwise stated.
English translation by Colin Partridge (Alderney/2010)

Cover: A 38 cm gun of Battery *Todt* at Audinghen in the Nord-Pas-de-Calais.
Today, one of these casemates houses a museum of the Atlantic Wall.

 – ISBN : 978-2-9533841-2-3 – EAN : 9782953384123
Editions Le Grand Blockhaus – Côte Sauvage – 44740 Batz-sur-Mer
www.grand-blockhaus.com – e-mail : grand-blockhaus@wanadoo.fr
Dépôt Légal 1er semestre 2010 – Imprimeries SPEI (Pulnoy)

Contents

Foreword

The Atlantic Wall! My brother and I have known this expression since childhood when, each year, our family went on holiday to Brittany. We spent our time exploring the remains of the Atlantic Wall, full of mystery for children eager for adventure. The war was already long over for more than thirty years, but we always hoped to discover some treasures inside: for us that would comprise helmets, cartridges and still more! They were rare, but our visits to the works were rich in discoveries, notably when they still possessed their guns or frescoes painted by soldiers on their internal walls. Sadly, no one seemed to be able to explain to us the function of these complex buildings which had once been inhabited not so long ago… The sole reply to all our questions was invariably…"*It was the Germans*." We hope that the reader of this book will be helped in replying to those questions which we posed long ago on our travels along the Channel and Atlantic coasts: … "*Who conceived and constructed these works and how were they used ?*"

The 17 cm guns of Battery MII *at Sangatte were emplaced opposite the English coast during the summer of 1940* (Coll. BA).

The first coastal batteries face England

From 3rd September 1939, France and England were at war with Germany who had invaded Poland. On 8th April 1940, the German army attacked Denmark and Norway in northern Europe. On 10th May, the *Wehrmacht* went over to the offensive in the west in simultaneously attacking three neutral countries; Belgium, Holland and Luxembourg. The panzer divisions of *General* Guderian, crossing the forest of the Ardennes, penetrated the French frontier at Sedan on 13th May. The Dutch capitulated on 16th May, while the Germans traversed the Oise the following day. The Belgians, in their turn, capitulated on the night of 27th/28th May as the British began their evacuation of the greater part of their expeditionary force sent to France through the port of Dunkirk. Up to 4th June, 223,000 British were repatriated, as well as 112,000 French. It would take four years to achieve a landing in the reverse direction. The Germans crossed the Somme on 5th June and reached the Seine on the 9th.

Paris was declared an open city the following day by the French government, which had withdrawn to Tours and then Bordeaux…The same day, Italy declared war on France. The Germans entered Paris

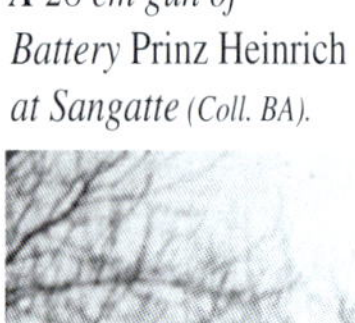

A 28 cm gun of Battery Prinz Heinrich *at Sangatte* (Coll. BA).

on 14th June and, three days later, Marshal Pétain made a radio broadcast to announce to the French people that negotiations for an armistice were taking place. It would be signed at Rethondes on 22nd June 1940. The French army, which had fought often with courage, lost 92,000 men and counted 125,000 wounded. In less than three months the Germans had conquered the entire Atlantic coastline from North Cape in Norway to the Spanish frontier.

On 2nd July 1940, the high command of the German army was charged with the preparation of a landing in England, which alone stood defiant: this was Operation SEALION. This landing would only be achievable if two preconditions were successful: total mastery of the air over the Channel to secure the crossing by the troops, and the prevention of the movement of heavy warships of the Royal Navy. While the aerial battle was fought out in the skies above the Channel, the German army brought up the long-range guns to the coastal sector between

In addition to the naval batteries, several 28 cm K5 *and* 21 cm K12 *railway guns of the army were transported to the Calais – Boulogne sector to protect the armada which would invade England, during its crossing of the Channel.*

***A** 30.5 cm gun of Battery* Friedrich August *at La Trésorerie (DR).*

***A**n 8.8 cm anti-air-craft gun protecting the Sangatte battery (Coll. AC).*

Rear view of a concrete casemate of Battery Todt *at Audinghen* (Coll. AC).

A mural inside one of the casemates at Battery Todt "Gegen Engeland" (Coll. AC).

Battery Todt *– a humorous fresco depicting Prime Minister Winston Churchill* (Coll. AC).

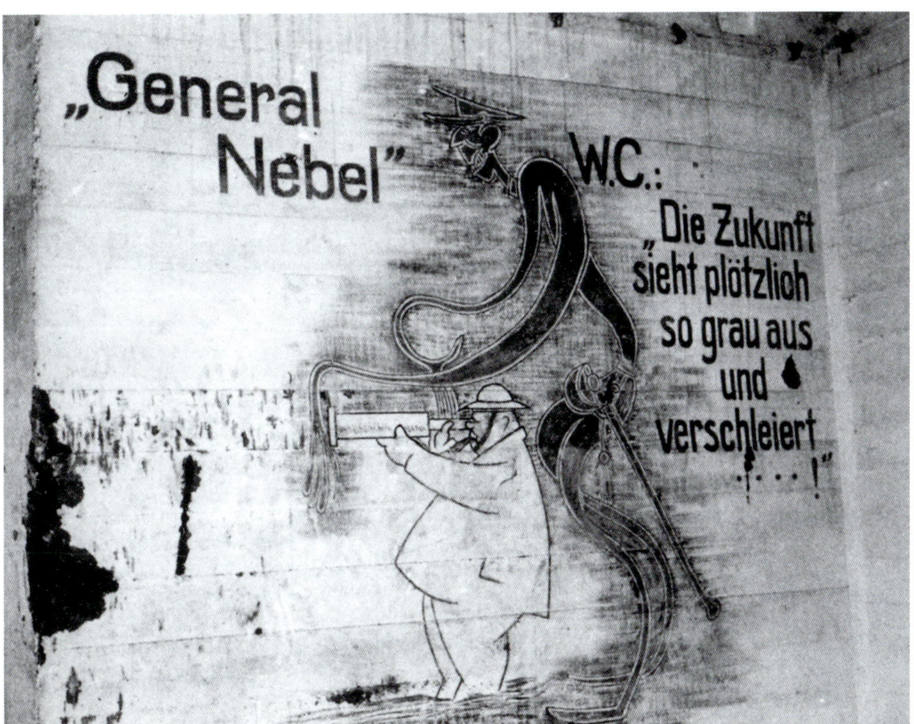

Boulogne-Calais; they were to control the maritime traffic in this narrowest part of the Channel where the German invasion was planned. These heavy artillery pieces, ranging in calibre from 24 cm up to 38 cm, were the first to be brought into action against England. The *Organisation Todt* would be charged with the protection of these five batteries under concrete casemates capable of resisting British bombs – they were the forerunners of a future gigantic line of fortifications…

The head of the Organisation Todt, *air force general Fritz* Todt *(Coll. AC).*

The Organisation Todt

Where did the *Organisation Todt* originate? On 5th July 1933, *Doctor* Fritz Todt, an engineer and former pilot of the 1914-18 war, had been appointed Inspector-General for German Road Construction. He was charged with directing the construction of an enormous network of motorways in Germany. In order to realise this ambitious project, 400,000 men had already been engaged since 1934. The name, *Organisation Todt*, appeared for the first time in 1938. The following year, on 1st March 1939, this army of workers had completed a total of 3,065 kms of motorways. But this was not the only task confided in the organisation of *Doctor* Fritz Todt: it was charged on 28th May 1938 with the construction of the Westwall, or Siegfried Line, the fortified line which would face the Maginot Line. On 1st September 1939, this defensive line extended some 630 kms and already comprised 13,700 bunkers. The *Organisation Todt* (*O.T.*), having taken its first steps in the military sphere, would go on to extend its field of activities throughout the European continent with the future invasions of the *Wehrmacht*. This paramilitary organisation, which possessed its own uniforms and particular ranks, was going to accompany the army while remaining wholly independent. Its role was: to direct all European building projects of a strategic nature; industrial and civil protection, systems of communication, hydro-electric works, various fortifications. In February 1940, Fritz Todt assumed the titles of responsibility for construction and armament: he was nominated successively as Inspector-General for Special Projects under the Four-Year Plan, and Reichs-Minister for Armament and Munitions.

The first engineers of the *O.T.* were committed to France from the end of the month of June 1940, some few days only after the arrival of the first *Wehrmacht* troops. From the summer of 1940, battalions of the naval coastal forces and anti-aircraft defence were sent from Germany to secure the major Channel and Atlantic ports, principally Brest, Lorient and Saint-Nazaire, chosen as the main strongpoints of the *Kriegsmarine*. Their guns would be protected by casemates with walls of 2 metres thickness constructed by the *Organisation Todt*. The former positions of the French navy, placed in the most strategic locations, were taken over. The old forts would find themselves surrounded by very modern bunkers, camouflaged by the ancient stonework to make them merge with their surroundings...

With regard to the question of command organisation, the French Atlantic coastline would be virtually divided into a dozen coastal sectors. Each coastal sector would correspond with a construction section of the *O.T.*, in general based in one of the large ports, and whose head would be responsible to the headquarters of the *O.T.* for France, the Netherlands and Belgium, the *OT-Einsatzgruppe West*. The offices of the latter were situated at 33/35 avenue Champs-Elysées, in Paris. This chain of command in the west, which would execute the construction projects in collaboration with the armed services, was directly subordinate to the *OT-Zentrale* under the command of Fritz Todt in Berlin.

The engineers of the *Organisation Todt* drew up the plans for the bunkers according to the construction specifications produced by the director of projects for the *Kriegsmarine* for the works destined for the navy and by the fortress engineers for the army: this engineer section was responsible for everything concerning fortifications. It was charged with selecting the emplacement of the batteries and the type of bunkers which would be constructed. Their specialists also decided if the bunkers to be built were to be of the types that could be found in the catalogue of plans (*Regelbauten*), or if it was necessary to construct a bunker adapted to the geographical considerations and tactical location which

Three members of the O.T. *read the journal dedicated to them,* "Der Forntarbeiter - *the front line worker";* *the cover of this number shows one of the casemates of the celebrated Battery* Todt, *nowadays visitable as a museum.*

produced a non-standard bunker (*Sonderkonstruction*). They also controlled the construction companies affiliated to the *O.T.* during the course of the project to ensure that the work conformed to standard. They inspected the works once completed. Finally, these sections formed the various units for the use of special materials involved in the Atlantic Wall.

In order to pour the foundations of a future casemate, the O.T. *workers have lined up several concrete mixers.*

The old Vauban fort at Martray, constructed in the centre of the Ile de Ré at its narrowest point, has been re-used by the O.T. who have modernized it by integrating an offensive casemate, one gun emplacement and Tobruk pits for a machine gun (coll. SHM).

The troops destined to occupy a position were, in general, assembled over six weeks in the same barracks where the fortress engineer unit was billeted. The fortress engineer park stored the various internal components destined to be fitted in the casemates. One existed for each construction section. The headquarters of the engineers was similarly charged with the ordering of materials from the major German companies such as Anton Piller and Auer. Once installed within the bunker, the engineers remained responsible for ensuring the functioning of the doors, hinges, etc. …and their maintenance.

The *Organisation Todt* was also charged from early in the year 1941 with the construction of the three gigantic bases for the protection of submarines at Brest, Lorient and Saint-Nazaire. In September, the works for the other submarine bases would commence at La Rochelle and Bordeaux, as well as Bergen and Trondheim in Norway. For the construction of the two bases situated south of the Loire, the majority of the work force was provided by former Spanish republican refugees in France after the Spanish Civil War: 10,000 were engaged in the northern zone, 30,000 in the southern zone. Bases were also provided for fast motor boats in Holland and Belgium, as well as at Dunkirk, Boulogne, Le Havre and Cherbourg. If the major ports were fortified and well defended, there still remained the question in mid-1941 of a line of continuous defence on the Atlantic…The greatest battery of the Atlantic Wall also saw the light of day during the summer at Cap Blanc Nez, facing England: this was Battery *Lindemann*, armed with powerful 40,6 cm guns.

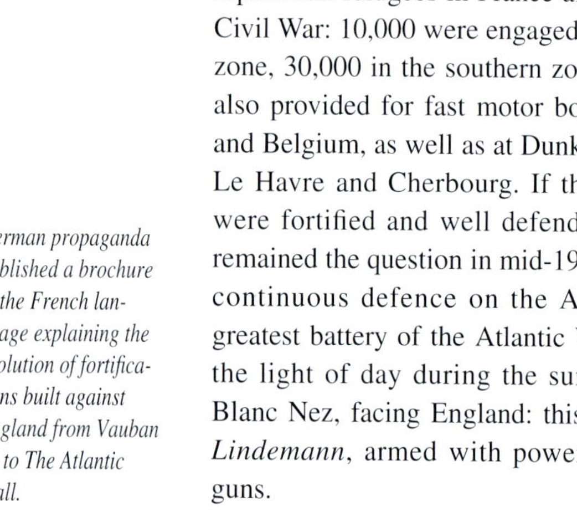

German propaganda published a brochure in the French language explaining the evolution of fortifications built against England from Vauban up to The Atlantic Wall.

German troops at the alert on the dunes behind a network of barbed wire (Coll. AC).

The birth of the Atlantic Wall

The *Luftwaffe*, having failed to secure mastery of the air above the Channel, being repulsed without break, the project for the invasion of Great Britain was postponed indefinitely on 12th October 1940. The troops massed in northern France to carry it out were progressively transferred to the east… On 22nd June 1941, supported by Finnish, Hungarian and Romanian forces, the *Wehrmacht* attacked Russia, reaching the suburbs of Moscow in December. Following the Japanese attack on Pearl Harbor on 7th December 1941, Germany and Italy declared war on the United States on 11th December. It was exactly three days later that the expression "Atlantic Wall" was first mentioned by Hitler. This rampart, which he wanted to be impregnable, was intended to protect Fortress Europe from any invasion coming from the west. Germany envisaged the European coastline as the bulwarks of a ship and placed its defences there. It wanted to retain the occupied countries in which it had imposed its moral order and prevent absolutely the opening of a second front as in 1914-18. To protect its empire in the west, the German high command charged the *Organisation Todt* with the creation of its greatest work: an impenetrable line of defence which would extend from the Franco-Spanish frontier as far as the north of Norway, more than 6,000 kms of coastline! On 20th October, the coast was declared a strategic zone by the superior military command in France: only civilians whose place of permanent residence was there were allowed to remain, supplied with a special permit from the *Kommandantur*. All others would be

The most common defence work, the Tobruk *pit for an* MG34, *in its anti-aircraft version* (Coll. AC).

Former French soldiers coming from North Africa were not sent to Germany ; they were transformed into work battalions ; Pointe des Espagnols, Brest.

moved out by 10th November and could only return if they were successful in obtaining special authorization. To equip this wall, the Germans were going to reuse the considerable armament which they had seized following their successive campaigns in Czechoslovakia, Poland, Belgium, Holland, then France. But that would not suffice: they would also relocate the guns formerly found on their Baltic Sea coastline!

To assist in this gigantic Atlantic Wall construction enterprise, the *O.T.* utilised to the full private German building companies and those of the occu-

A Renault R35 *tank turret has been reused in a fixed position at St-Gilles-de-Vie in Vendée* (coll. BA).

A battery fire-direction post camouflaged by the zebras (Coll. AC).

A 5 cm anti-tank gun in a concrete emplacement faces the beach.

pied countries. They exchanged building contracts with the companies and acted in a supervisory capacity in assuring the supply of materials and plant. As many as 200 large German contractors would be employed in the west. These large firms, once contracted to the *O.T.*, could sub-contract with the smaller German and foreign specialists. All French enterprises – masonry, joinery, electrical, plumbing, painting – interested the *O.T.* For the workers, their mode of life was unchanged: those who worked for the French companies contracted to the *O.T.* were subject to the same laws, and were always paid by their employer. In addition, from January 1941, several hundred French prisoners-of-war in Germany were repatriated to France: these were specialists in building and public works. They would join several dozen thousand colonial troops of the French army, principally North-Africans taken prisoner in May-June 1940, on the many construction sites; in fact, they had not been sent to Germany, but detained in *Frontstalags* in France ready to be formed into work commandos.

In this Tobruk *pit for an 8 cm mortar at La Baule, the targets have been painted directly on the internal walls.*

The most common army battery fire-direction post, with construction number R636 *in the bunker catalogue of the* O.T. *; Battery* Chiberta *at Les Landes.*

Autumn 1941, the Organisation Todt *completes the formwork to the powerful 40.6 cm turrets of Battery* Lindemann *in the Pas-de-Calais.*

But how was the *O.T.* able to pay for all these materials, these contractors and workers? In France, it was the French who paid! In fact, according to the conventions of the armistice of 22nd June 1940, the French state daily poured a colossal sum into the German administration – the dues of occupation. These 400 million francs given daily, normally capable of providing for the maintenance for the occupation forces in France, in fact contributed largely to the construction of the Atlantic Wall. Around 1,500 French construction companies would directly for the *O.T.* on the Atlantic Wall in France. The liaison and protection service for the French companies working for the *O.T.* was charged with the coordination of projects. There were two categories of companies: those who worked actively for the *O.T.* in soliciting contracts and whose sole objective was to obtain the maximum benefits; amongst this category was found the numerous "mushroom" enterprises created for the occasion. The other French companies also worked for the *O.T.*, for it was the only authority, but without zeal and with the single purpose of preserving their ability to work. One group of the "mushroom" companies was a sort of wholesalers whose job consisted of sourcing diverse materials such as pickaxes, shovels, wheelbarrows, bolts, electrical cables, steel reinforcement, shuttering timber…and of their re-sale in bulk at a good price to the *O.T.*, which was a very great consumer.

A German language pamphlet, "The Steel Coast", *intended to reassure German civilians and the military of the strength of the Atlantic Wall.*

As a practical technician and former officer in the war of 1914-18, *Doctor* Fritz Todt thought from the end of 1941 that Germany could not win the war. He was one of the few high- ranking German officials who attempted to convince Hitler that it was time to stop. He tried to do so in Berlin on 29th November 1941, and Hitler put an end to the discussion. Fritz Todt retained his positions. A new, heated discussion took place at Rastenburg on 7th February 1942. But the very next morning, Fritz Todt was dead: the aircraft which was carrying him back to Berlin crashed shortly after take-off. Xaver Dorsch replaced him as head of *OT-Zentrale*, with Albert Speer filling his ministerial posts. These men were easier for Hitler to manipulate than Todt, who had a much stronger personality. At this time in France, the *O.T.* numbered 112,00 Germans and 152,000 French, of whom 17,000 were North-Africans.

In the east, the *Wehrmacht* was fighting over an immense front. To compensate for the human losses, all the German services were required to make a contribution. The *O.T.* would lose its younger German elements: on 1st January 1942, it would relinquish 4,167 men to the *Wehrmacht* of the 1917-1922 age group; on 1st February, 2,898 from the 1913-1916 age group; on 1st May, 4,057 more of the 1911-1912 group and on 1st July, 1,820 men born in 1910. The transfers continued in 1943 to such effect that the *O.T.* would call on a female workforce to fill the posts of secretaries, accountants, telephonists…

Directive No.40 of the German high command of 23rd March 1942 set out the main principles of the Atlantic Wall: The coastline of Europe will, in a very large measure in the months to come, be exposed to the danger of enemy landings. In the event, the date and place of the enemy's landing operations will not be dictated solely by operational considerations. Setbacks in other operational theatres, engagements in support of the Allied cause, and political considerations could persuade him to take decisions which appear unlikely from the purely military point of view. Even enemy landing operations with a limited objective, where they result in the enemy establishing a foothold on the coast, will interfere seriously with our own intentions. They will interrupt our own maritime traffic in coastal waters and engage important forces of the army and air force which would have to be withdrawn from

Tubular steel bed-frames in a hospital bunker at Lorient.

decisive theatres of operations. A special danger presents itself should the enemy succeed in capturing our airfields or establishing his own airfields in the areas that he has conquered. The important military installations which support the war effort, which are often established on the coast or in the immediate neighbourhood, some of which are equipped with very valuable materiel, may offer moreover a great attraction for local surprise operations. One should also specially observe the English preparations for landing operations on the coast, operations for which the enemy possesses numerous landing craft equipped to carry tanks and heavy weapons. One should also take account of the possibility of airborne and parachute operations on a large scale.

This directive, which marked the actual birth of the Atlantic Wall, also defined the combat instructions for the different services: for the navy, the air force and the army, as well as the powers of the commanders. Reconnaissance for an attack would be provided jointly by radar, ships of the *Kriegsmarine* and aircraft of the *Luftwaffe*; discovery of such operations would be the principal task of the intelligence services. All of the troops stationed on the Atlantic Wall would be trained for the purpose and armed in order to be able to participate in combat; no person would be authorised to withdraw to the rear and would assist in throwing the attacker back into the sea. The army was charged with the defence of the coastline between the ports, and would be organised into strongpoints capable of all-round defence. Each fortified position would be adequately provided with ammunition, reserves of water and food to hold out during a prolonged battle. The army would establish infantry strongpoints directly on the shoreline, and its artillery batteries some kilometres inland in order to direct fire on an attacker who had already landed. The command should be unified, principally for the major ports where a commander would be responsible for the entire defence.

The German troops would take refuge in bunkers with walls of 2 metres thickness, which would serve to shelter a machine gun, a mortar, a flame-thrower or a gun… Wherever possible, these bunkers would be underground, camouflaged with nets and even disguised as villas! The bunkers were chosen from a catalogue of over 800 types, each serving a particular purpose: for every type of gun, for a command post, for a hospital, for a personnel shelter, for an electrical generator, for ammunition storage, for reserves of food and water…where this was not possible, when the ground was particularly uneven or beyond the ability of the local architects of the *Organisation Todt*, the creation of a suitable bunker required a unique design.

Casemate for a Czech Skoda 4.7cm *gun – German Occupation Museum, Guernsey.*

Concrete shelter of the port commander at Le Havre.

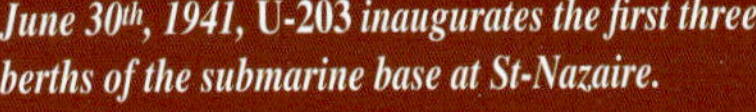

June 30th, 1941, **U-203** *inaugurates the first three berths of the submarine base at St-Nazaire.*

Spring 1941, a U-boat *is slid into a* **Dom-Bunker** *at Lorient.*

Interior of the fast patrol boat base at Cherbourg.

A mural showing the construction of the St-Nazaire base in a restaurant requisitioned by the Organisation Todt.

Parade of the Lorient submarine base garrison before the camouflaged berths of Kéroman II *which allows the U-boats to be serviced on dry land.*

A mural of a submarine conning tower painted in the base at Saint-Nazaire.

In August 1941, U-123 *is the first submarine to be dry-docked in the* Kéroman I *base.*

The *NSKK* provides the transport

Created in 1931, well before the war, the paramilitary organisation, the *NSKK* (*National Sozialistisches Kraftfahr Korps*) had, as its principle objective, to train the civilian motorised transport, to give pre-military instruction to its members and, above all, to provide the future recruits for the motorised and armoured units of the army. The *NSKK* troops began working with the *Organisation Todt* from September 1938 with the construction of the Siegfried Line. The *O.T.* lacked not only vehicles, but above all drivers and mechanics trained to carry construction materials, tools and also to bring the workers to the building sites. The head of the *NSKK*, *Reichsleiter* Hühnlein, provided these means to the *O.T.*: 15,000 lorries for the transport of materials and 5,000 buses to bring 200,000 men daily to the building sites. After the French campaign, the *NSKK* would participate in the construction of the Atlantic Wall by supplying the means of transport to the *O.T.* The *NSKK* drivers allotted to the *O.T.* constituted a special corps formed into regiments, battalions, companies and sections: the *NSKK* Transport-Brigade-Todt. Since its arrival in France, the officials of the *NSKK* bought, hired or requisitioned thousands of vehicles of every type, as well as garages. The *NSKK* lorry and bus park in France numbered some 8,000 vehicles, 95% of which were of French origin. Of note also was the existence of the *NSKK Transport-Brigade-Speer*, more active in support of the *Luftwaffe* in the construction of airfields and bunkers.

Its officials were also charged with setting up groups of non-German volunteer personnel. The first to be integrated with the *NSKK* in 1941 were the Dutch and Flemish volunteers. The *NSKK Transport-Brigade-Todt* would extend its recruitment in 1942 to the Latins, with the integration of Walloon and French volunteers. The French, aged between 18 and 50 years, were recruited by means of small advertisements and posters to work in the *NSKK*. In Paris, the recruiting office was directed by Captain Troupeau, brother-in-law of the war minister, General Eugène Bridoux. Those who signed up were required to make a declaration of faith and wear a uniform with the French national emblem on the left arm. Drivers earned 45 Reichsmarks per week, excluding overtime or Sunday work; they benefited from 14-days leave every six months. The minimum period of engagement was two years. One driving school was opened at Melun in Seine-et-Marne. The French of North-African origin were also accepted in the *NSKK*, which was not the case of Russian émi-

Truppführer *Schuh, chief of* Hauptkolonne 8 *of the* NSKK-Transport-Brigade-Todt, *who can be seen wearing the brassard denoting this rank, has received the Merit Cross for his action during the Allied raid on Dieppe.*

ORGANISATION TODT
Einsatzgruppe West
Az.: 4152 P. 42
Aktenzeichen bei Antwort angeben.
NSKK-Kraftwagenleitung

Unit letter-heading of the NSKK-Transport-Brigade-Todt *carrying the stamp of the* Organisation Todt *western command.*

grés in France after 1917; while the latter could enter into a separate civil contract as drivers for the *O.T.*, they could not wear the uniform. Around 5,000 French would serve in the *NSKK* during the war. On 22nd July 1942, the two transport brigades of *Todt* and *Speer* were reformed into a single group, the *NSKK Transportgruppe Todt*. Foreigners who could not become members of the *NSKK* would be integrated to form a new, more combat-orientated group, the *Legion Speer*; it would be engaged notably in Hungary and northern Italy.

In October 1942, these two corps numbered in the whole of Europe some 70,000 drivers and legionnaires with a park of 50,000 vehicles. As the *NSKK* was a logistical support unit, the troops of the first line translated the initials *NSKK* as "*Nicht Schiessen! Kein Kämpfer!*" , which means "*Don't shoot! Non-combatants!*". The French in the *NSKK*, for their part, referred to the unit under the title of "*Coin-Coin!*". The last two letters of their formation "*KK*" recalled the time when the sound of the klaxon, shaped like a pear, was fitted to old vehicles.

French members of the NSKK, *one of whom in the centre can be seen wearing the blue, white, red emblem on the arm, setting up the* V1 *installations at Crécy-en-Ponthieu in 1944.*

A moment always dreaded by the troops, the battery review !

This NCO of the coast artillery, serving in Cherbourg, is the oldest soldier in the Kriegsmarine *in which his son and grandsons also serve ! He is surrounded by women naval auxiliaries.*

The artillery of the Navy

At the beginning of the Second World War, German naval artillery comprised only six divisions. The personnel in these units, stationed on the defences of the German Baltic and North Sea coasts, was clearly insufficient to provide the units for the future batteries of the Atlantic Wall, which extended from the north of Norway to the Spanish frontier. It was therefore necessary to recruit thousands of reservists and mobilizable young men. The recruitment of personnel for the coast artillery always played second place to other departments of the navy. Little by little, this effectively reduced the standard of troops, so that by 1944 it was a corps of very average value.

In particular, the body of officers in the coast artillery was not an elite corps, and was disdained by the sea-going officers. In fact, the *Kriegsmarine* placed those who served in the larger warships and especially in the submarine arm above all others. The mission of defending the coast was considered of little glory and of less importance by comparison with the offensive actions engaged in by ships of the *Kriegsmarine* at sea. For this reason, the body of officers in the naval artillery was, in the very great majority, composed of reservists amongst whom were former combatants of the 1914-18 war. To fill the available places, numerous young NCOs were promoted as aspiring battery commanders. The troops, for their part, were constantly solicited to serve at sea. The youngest and the most motivated, attracted by the propaganda, were first to leave. The submarine arm would swallow up the majority of the young gunners. From 1942, the greater number of troops under the age of 35 were automatically replaced by much older personnel. The latter were often drafted to batteries without any prior instruction. They were expected to learn on site, but the low stocks of ammunition and the lack of boats

The entrance to the command post of the 804 Naval Flak Battalion, installed in a château in the Brest sector, has been enhanced by two old French coast defence guns, the Lahitolle model 1888.

A troop review at Brest for these soldiers of the Marineflak*; those in the middle are wearing tunics without pockets !*

which could serve as target tugs often prevented the authorisation of practice shoots. Thos troops who had acquired a good knowledge of the equipment were constantly replaced. As a result, specialists were rare. As there were always more batteries under construction, it was necessary to send the capable personnel there to train the new recruits. As time passed, more of the specialists were submerged among poorly qualified personnel.

The anti-aircraft brigades of the navy, responsible for the defence of the major ports of Brest, Lorient and Saint-Nazaire, were however very efficient: each one was composed of five battalions formed by six batteries equipped with guns ranging from 2 cm to 12.8 cm…

A 24 cm railway gun at Batz-sur-Mer ; it consists of French colonial guns, model 1893/1896 captured by the Germans in 1940.

Kriegsmarine *recruits trained at the close-combat school of Pierre-Attelée at St-Brévin in 1942 ; the majority of them appear quite old, though not in the case of the two soldiers to the right of the front rank !*

The German magazine "Die Kriegsmarine" of May 1942 shows a naval gun in the St-Nazaire sector on the cover.

An adjutant in the naval coastal artillery, the "Spiess", with his NCO's cap.

A booklet issued to those serving in the anti-aircraft defence for recognition of the types of enemy aircraft.

A 34 cm gun of the Bégot Battery at Plouharnel protecting the Lorient sector.

Naval artilleryman Karl Draschdil, seen here on leave, was a Czechoslovak enrolled in the **Kriegsmarine** *– he would be posted to Lorient then Saint-Nazaire, where he remained after the war.*

The paybook of a naval artilleryman of Czech origin at St-Brévin; it carries the reference "Personalliste St-Nazaire" followed by a number confirming that he has been in this fortress after August 1944.

The command post of **V.Marine-Flak-Brigade** *at Saint-Marc-sur-Mer near St-Nazaire. A gigantic underground bunker for the direction of anti-aircraft operations is surmounted by an observation tower and mess.*

A 2 cm gun in place in the Saint-Nazaire sector with its crew and the range-taker on the right, charged with calculating the distance of the target.

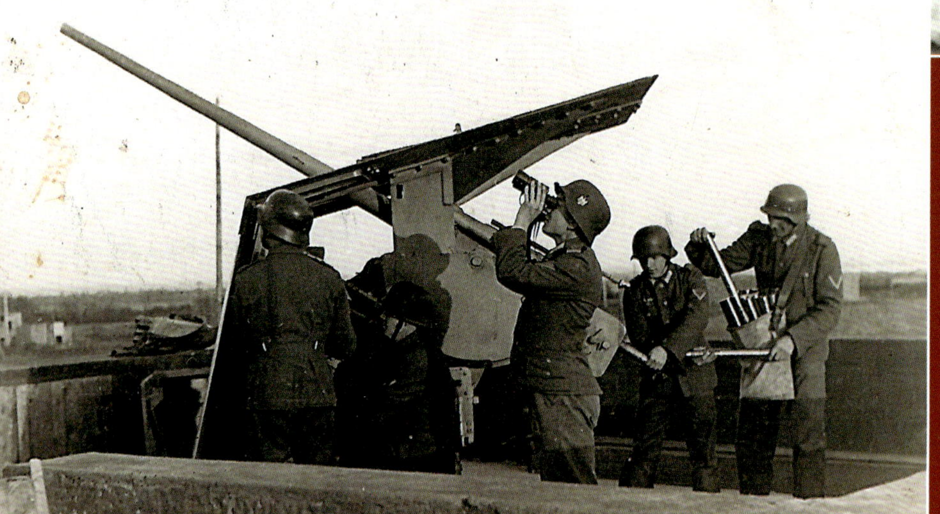

A 3.7 cm anti-aircraft gun and its crew ; to the right the ammunition handler.

The 10.5 cm anti-aircraft battery at Kerlédé near Saint-Nazaire. Installed on the sea front, it could also engage a naval target if necessary.

A 12.8 cm anti-aircraft gun of the Drache naval Flak *battery in the Saint-Nazaire sector.*

A twin 10.5 cm anti-aircraft gun at St-Brévin in the St-Nazaire sector.

This British bomber, hit by Flak in 1942, crashed at Trignac near St-Nazaire.

A soldier of the naval artillery, set for guard duty, leaves for his patrol – Le Grand Blockhaus at Batz-sur-Mer.

A soldier, qualified as a specialist in range-finding, makes his report on a typewriter ; his cap bears a starfish, the emblem of the battery at Raversijde in Belgium.

The battery commander's room at Raversijde has been faithfully recreated ; the trunk containing his personal effects, all marked with his name, was recovered a few years ago in a nearby farm.

Undoubtedly the accordéon offered by Field Marshal *Rommel as a reward to the personnel of this well-maintained and camouflaged battery – Raversijde.*

The chief armourer of the battery ; identifiable on the wall are five P08s, *five* P38s *and four* MP40s *– Raversijde.*

Troops quarters recreated at the Museum of Le Grand Blockhaus with a nurse of the German Red Cross.

This naval artilleryman is equipped with apparatus for the transmission of orders – Raversijde.

Under the surveillance of an Admiral *and the battery chief at Raversijde, an administrative officer uses a three-rotor* Enigma *machine to send a coded message.*

The battery commander's room in Le Grand Blockhaus – in the centre is an officer of the RAD *– the German Labour Service.*

While one soldier stands guard, the others rest in the shelter of a bunker surmounted by a steel observation cupola - Le Touquet (Coll. BA).

The daily life of troops on the Wall

A typical day for German troops in the batteries resembled the life experienced earlier by French soldiers on the Maginot Line. They awoke at 07.00 hours and began by tidying their quarters. After washing, everyone took breakfast with malted coffee. At 08.00 hours was the daily roll call for inspection at the appointed station, followed by each one taking leave for their allotted daily task. At 12.00 hours, the midday roll call was followed by the report of the unit adjutant, the Spiess. A meal then followed. Daily duties were resumed from 14.00 to 18.00 hours: once a week the cleaning of weapons and sporting activities were undertaken. Dinner was taken at 18.00 hours and free time followed for most of the crews. Soldiers could go out up to 22.00 hours, NCOs up to 23.00 hours and officers all night if they wished. The possibilities for those who remained permanently in the battery were: writing a diary, playing cards, draughts or chess, ping-pong or billiards in the mess, reading, listening to music, making models. Certain artists spent their time decorating their mess or bunkers with wall paintings. Often, those who worked on the land before the war supplemented their rations by growing vegetables in a small garden close to their barracks.

Crew room on the Atlantic Wall, decorated with photographs of the sailors' wives.

One officer played a primary role: that was the battery chief. His very diverse tasks concerned at the same time the operational direction of the battery and the daily management of the hundred or so men under his orders. At the operational level, he was required to organise his men's duties on a daily basis. He was charged with maintaining the troops at the highest state of readiness, particularly by organising combat exercises. The troops must be ready, by day or night, to fulfil the role for which they have been formed. Exercises also permitted a break in the routine which characterised the service, and contribu-

This artilleryman has made a doll's wardrobe during his spare time.

ted to preventing a relaxation in the vigilance of the troops. In the event of a real attack, the battery chief is responsible for the command to open fire. Before giving the order to open fire, he would consult his gunnery officer, often a lieutenant, assisted by two NCO specialists who supplied him with details of the technical information and general situation. After firing the first salvo, the battery chief examines the results through his binoculars and can ask for fire to be corrected. The same routine follows each salvo. He is also the person who gives the order to cease fire.

As regards the welfare of the men, the battery chief must deal with the paperwork of the unit. He alone validates the papers with the battery's own stamp which he must, at all times, secure under lock in a safe or cabinet. To manage the entire administrative life of the unit, he is not alone however. He has an office at his disposal with several secretaries under the orders of an NCO. The latter also acts as the paymaster in distributing pay once a month. The battery chief may also propose technical training and external courses for his men if he considers it necessary. He may also send soldiers to follow group education and thus obtain promotion. In observing the conduct of his men under fire, he has the opportunity to recommend them for a decoration. If such is approved by his superiors, he is able to organise a small official ceremony for its presentation. If he was able to reward a soldier for his good conduct, he could also punish him for a misdemeanour in ordering up to three days arrest. For a serious act of indiscipline, the soldier could be sent before a military tribunal. He could send soldiers on leave if there was no alert in the region. To ensure that the battery always remained at operational readiness with a minimum of troops, it was necessary to balance the numbers of soldiers who were unfit with those on leave. The battery chief would also keep an eye on the morale of his troops, amongst whom were those who determined the spirit of the crew. In order to prevent the troops from squabbling, he could find some distractions in their spare time. He could generally make available a small area of land beside the battery with the object of organising football matches and various other sports. He could arrange for his paymaster to purchase books for the battery library. He could motivate those with different hidden talents to organise theatrical events or cabaret, as well as musical evenings which were often arranged on the occasion of birthdays or anniversaries such as Christmas, New Year's Day…

These artillerymen have slipped into their white working overalls to carry out some painting – Pointe des Espagnols, Brest.

The little orchestra for the Flak *battery at Méan-Penhoët near Saint-Nazaire.*

An artilleryman of Marine-Flak-Abteilung 804 *at Brest plays the accordéon to entertain his comrades.*

A naval officer of the coast artillery, has changed into his blue leave uniform to buy a Tune ice-cream in La Baule.

A contemporary photograph entitled "Humour".

Olympic games of the Kriegsmarine *at La Baule during the summer of '43 – each battery has sent its best athletes to take part.*

This naval officer (Maat) proudly displays the Iron Cross on his tunic.

A review for these soldiers is held in front of the concrete entrance to a tunnel in Normandy named "Hermann's Hole" (Coll. BA).

Mural in the sick bay.

An underground room in the tunnels at Auderville in Normandy (Coll. BA).

An artist has painted this humorous mural on the wall of a bunker : it takes the form of a gun called "the miracle machine" which transforms the recalcitrants into disciplined, goose-stepping soldiers !

A celebration in a concrete shelter among infantry and armoured troops (Coll. AC).

An artilleryman painted a fresco in which he holds a portrait of his fiancée – Le Grand Blockhaus.

NAHKAMPF

Mural in Dieppe : "Close combat".

The fire-direction post of Battery des Arros at Soulac.

Christmas in a crew room on the Atlantic Wall : everyone is keen to open their presents (Coll. AC).

A nurse of the German Red Cross distributes books to this soldier manning a tank turret in a permanent position on the Atlantic Wall (Coll. AC).

A casemate for a Skoda 4.7 cm gun camouflaged to integrate it within an old castle at Roscoff (Coll. BA).

At St-Nazaire on the morning of March 28th, 1942, some hours before it exploded, the destroyer Campbeltown *is embedded in the lock gate enclosing the Joubert dock.*

The two Allied raids on the ports of Saint-Nazaire and Dieppe

On 6th June 1940, only two days after the embarkation of British forces at Dunkirk, Winston Churchill gave his approval for raids on the enemy coasts by one or several small groups of well-armed and trained men. The idea of the Commandos was born. The first symbolic "test" raid was carried out by 120 soldiers on the night of 23rd/24th June 1940 on the Channel Island of Guernsey occupied by the Germans, but no enemy was seen. A large commando unit was formed using new training methods, taking the name of the Special service Brigade. Training was very intensive, notably that which consisted of disembarking from specialised landing craft. The first significant raid by British commandos took place on the Lofoten Islands in north-west Norway on 4th March 1941. A second raid was mounted with Canadian troops against a group of islands in the north of Norway in September 1941. Other actions were organised in North Africa, notably a failed attempt to assassinate General Rommel. On 27th October 1941, Lord Mountbatten assumed the command of Combined Operations whose objective was to co- ordinate the action of land, air and sea forces. He mounted his first raid, more audacious than those which preceded it, on 27th December 1941: the object was the port of Vaagso in Norway; this was a success. The following raid was carried out on the French coast on the night of 27th/28th February 1942: commandos were parachuted behind the German radar station at Bruneval, where they dismantled the essential parts and withdrew by sea.

The first truly important raid, against the port of Saint-Nazaire, was carried out by 600 men during the night of 27th/28th March 1942. It occurred less than a week after the appearance of the German directive No.40 which predicted what it feared – "*surprise enemy landing operations against military installations on the coast*"! After a diversionary bombardment, an entire flotilla penetrated the port of Saint-Nazaire under German defensive fire. A destroyer packed with explosives was rammed into the gate of the largest dry dock on the Atlantic coast, where the battleship *Tirpitz* would have been able to seek refuge in case of damage. The commandos successfully destroyed several port installations, but were unable to penetrate the submarine base. The British would suffer the loss of two-thirds of their

Reconstruction of the British raid on St-Nazaire : two wounded commandos have taken refuge in a shelter – Le Grand Blockhaus.

force. The raid on Saint- Nazaire would be proclaimed by Churchill as "*one of the greatest feats of arms of the entire Second World War*". The German and French newspapers, both censored, spoke only of the British losses and forgot to mention that the repair dock had been well and truly destroyed…

The Russians, who were suffering very heavy losses, demanded with insistence that the Americans and British open a second front in the west to take the German army in the rear. The Germans had anticipated it in their directive No.40 in stating "*engagements in support of the Allied cause, and political considerations could persuade him to take decisions which appear unlikely from the purely military point of view.*" The Allies were planning a still more important raid at the very moment that the Germans launched their second summer offensive on the eastern front. Carried out against the port of Dieppe on 19th August 1942, this attempted landing would

Reconstruction of the British raid : a sailor and three commandos having taken refuge in a civilian shelter in St-Nazaire prepare to return to the assault – Le Grand Blockhaus.

On March 28th, 1942, British commandos have been held prisoner on a minesweeper in the basin in front of the submarine base at Saint-Nazaire.

turn into a catastrophe… Of the 6,000 troops engaged, mostly Canadians, less than half would return to England.

German propaganda would exploit its success to the maximum with the two raids carried out by the British and Canadians at Saint-Nazaire and Dieppe, with the expression "*Never two without three.*" However, on the strategic level, the consequence of these raids which harassed the Germans was to force them into increasing the number of men present in the sectors of secondary importance. The attack on Dieppe also demonstrated to the Allies that they would have to bypass a large port in their future invasion… Numerous other raids would be mounted up to mid-1944, but only with small groups of commandos.

Following these two raids, and believing that the Allies would have need of a large port to land their equipment, the Germans decided as a priority to fortify all the large coastal ports. They would not only be well-defended on the seaward face, but also protected on the landward side by a defensive system comprising hundreds of bunkers manned by the army and directed towards the rear. Between these ports, the defences would be considerably less for the Germans did not have the means to defend 6,000 kms of coastline effectively. Believing that the Allies, when launching their assault, would concentrate all of their forces at a single point and, inspired by the old adage that "*he who would defend everything defends nothing*", they gave absolute priority in August 1942 to the protection of the major ports.

Crew members of motor launch ML306, *several of whom were wounded, are taken prisoner at Saint-Nazaire.*

Unused British demolition materials recovered by the Germans in the port at St-Nazaire.

Gebetsandenken
an den gefallenen Krieger
Karl Seitz
Zimmermannssohn von Flossing
Marine-Artillerist
welcher am 28. März 1942, bei dem Angriff der Engländer auf St. Nazaire (Frankreich), im Alter von 20 1/4 Jahren den Heldentod fürs Vaterland starb.

Eine Kugel spitz und hart
Schickte mich auf meine letzte Fahrt.
Die Fahrt geht zum Himmel hin,
Da ist mein lieber Bruder drinn;
Er wartet schon auf mich.
Mutter, trockne Deine Tränen.
Als mich traf das kalte Erz,
War bei Dir mein letztes Sehnen,
Brich nicht mein liebes Mutterherz.

H. Stocker, Mühldorf

Death notice of a naval artilleryman following the assault by British commandos on the port of Saint-Nazaire on March 28th, 1942.

At the beginning of April 1942, the Germans bury their dead from the raid on St-Nazaire at Pornichet.

At the beginning of April 1942, the Germans extend military honours to the dead commandos buried at La Baule-Escoublac ; second from the left is Otto Koch, who will be one of the few survivors of the dreadful battle for the Ile de Cézembre in August '44.

On the sea front at St-Nazaire, **Kapitän-zur-See** *Mecke,* **Flak** *commander of the St-Nazaire sector, receives the Knight's Cross for having identified the British attack.*

The French magazine, "Toute la Vie", relates the story of the British raid on St-Nazaire.

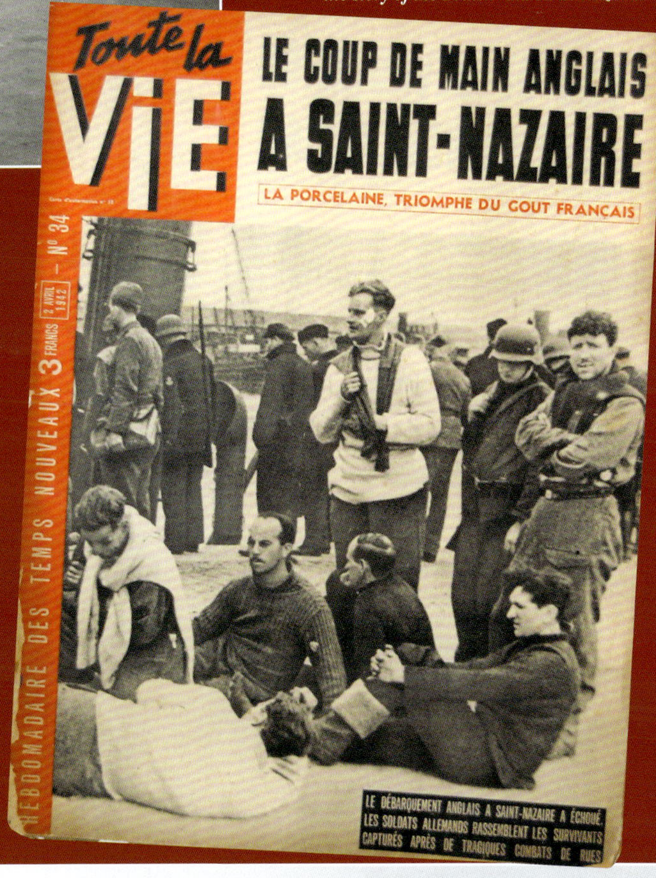

Toute la VIE

LE COUP DE MAIN ANGLAIS
A SAINT-NAZAIRE

LA PORCELAINE, TRIOMPHE DU GOUT FRANÇAIS

HEBDOMADAIRE DES TEMPS NOUVEAUX 3 FRANCS 2 AVRIL 1942 — N° 34

LE DÉBARQUEMENT ANGLAIS A SAINT-NAZAIRE A ÉCHOUÉ. LES SOLDATS ALLEMANDS RASSEMBLENT LES SURVIVANTS CAPTURÉS APRÈS DE TRAGIQUES COMBATS DE RUES

PREMIERES PHOTOS DE
LA TENTATIVE ANGLAISE
DE SAINT-NAZAIRE

PREMIER RÉCIT DE LA BATAILLE DE RANGOON
(Voir pages 6-7)

DES BRITANNIQUES RECUEILLIS EN MER SONT DÉBARQUÉS

12 AVRIL 1942 2 fr. 50

The French magazine, **"7 Jours"**, *under German control, reports* **"the British attempt"**.

Grand Admiral *Raeder, commander-in-chief of the* **Kriegsmarine**, *has come to award decorations to members of the coast artillery after the raid on St-Nazaire –* **Obergefreiter** *Lammert receives the Iron Cross 2nd Class.*

The British tanks have made little progress on the shingle beach at Dieppe.

British tanks destroyed in the raid on Dieppe on August 19th, 1942.

A member of the **NSKK-Transport-Brigade-Todt** *passes in front of a stricken tank at Dieppe ; a grounded ship can be seen behind it.*

Dieppe : Canadian soldiers carry one of their wounded on a stretcher.

Allied losses having been extremely heavy at Dieppe, it would be necessary to wait two more years before carrying out the Normandy landings.

A column of Canadian prisoners leaves for the prisoner-of-war camp.

Canadian soldiers taken prisoner at Dieppe.

While awaiting their transfer, these Canadian troops are guarded in front of a church in Dieppe.

DER SIEG VON DIEPPE

Der Strand von Dieppe, zwei Tage nach der Katastrophe der Briten. Hier fand der Hauptkampf statt.

19. AUGUST 1942

A German pamphlet on the failed attack on the port of Dieppe.

JAMAIS DEUX...

SANS TROIS...

The German slogan after the two raids, "Never two without three".

After the failed landing at Dieppe, German sailors bury their dead.

KAMPF-
AUF-
TRAG.

H.FELD
43

Painted mural in a bunker at Dieppe.

Anti-British tract addressed to the French people after the raids on St-Nazaire and Dieppe.

Commando scenario at Quinéville in December 1943, with the purpose of taking sections of beach obstacles for analysis - Mémorial de la Liberté retrouvée at Quinéville, Normandy.

Young recruits of the RAD *install barbed wire around the naval anti-aircraft battery at Kerlédé near St-Nazaire* (coll. ECPAD).

The *RAD* plays its part

On 26th June 1935, a service of obligatory work had been inaugurated in Germany. It involved all men between the age of 18 to 20 years. Who would be engaged under a strict regime of six months varied work for the state. The idea was to appreciate manual labour, to build up the character of the youth and to break down social barriers. Very quickly this service became an introduction to military life. Before the war, *RAD* units took part mainly in the creation of new agricultural land through the drainage of marshlands and clearance, but also in the construction of roads and various public works. From June 1938 to September 1939, around four hundred *RAD* companies assisted the *Organisation Todt* in the construction of fortifications: 300 companies in the west for the Siegfried Line, 100 in the east for the fortifications on the Polish frontier, the *Ostwall*. On the eve of the commencement of war in 1939, *RAD* personnel numbered some 360,000. A number of them was directly poured into army construction units the day after general mobilisation. The remainder became army auxiliaries in accompanying the combat units in their various campaigns. The *RAD* repaired and constructed bridges, railway tracks, aerodromes, roads and fortifications. From 1941, service in the *RAD* was reduced to three months.

The *RAD* played its part from the end of December 1942 in the establishment of the Atlantic Wall. Numerous camps of young Germans in the *RAD* were set up all along the Atlantic. Certainly, on account of their youth and their brassards, French civilians called them "Hitler Youth". They were not

Germans of the RAD *take part in clearing the view from this fire-direction post, type* R636, *of the army battery at La Chaume constructed by the* Organisation Todt *in the Sables d'Olonne sector, Vendée* (coll. BA).

directly involved in the pouring of concrete for the construction of bunkers, this complicated task being left to the engineers of the *O.T.* They were there above all to set up and protect the places where the troops were stationed: it was necessary to prepare the ground through clearing the positions, digging the foundations, erecting prefabricated barracks and camouflaging them, laying mines, digging trenches and erecting barbed wire… they could also camouflage the bunkers like the fortress engineers. Outside their activities on the Atlantic Wall and the maintenance of their camp, the *RAD* youth followed a course of general and ideological development, as well as of physical education. Spare time activities were organised at the end of the day. Their organisation was made up by former officers and NCOs having already completed their service. They were engaged voluntarily and were required to follow a preliminary course in a *RAD* school in Germany. The troops of the RAD would only be armed in 1943. As the German army began to lose manpower, a section of the *RAD* youth would be engaged to man the anti-aircraft batteries of the *Luftwaffe* – these were the *RAD-Flak* units. In August 1944, the members of the *RAD* who found themselves surrounded in the Atlantic Wall pockets would be directly absorbed into the infantry.

The German air force also contributed to the Atlantic Wall in providing batteries of 8.8 cm anti-aircraft guns outside the major ports defended by the navy.

The intensification of the works from the spring of 1942

From the spring of 1942, the works on the Atlantic Wall intensified. The *O.T.* opened new labour offices and embarked on a vast recruitment campaign to attract French and foreign workers with high salaries and various bonuses. The *O.T.* was forced to seek foreign recruits since Germans in the 1910-1925 age group were in great measure already absorbed by the army. Its manpower was considerably augmented. Volunteer workers benefited from various social advantages and had a guarantee of not being sent away. In November 1942, it was even decided to create a corps of social inspectors in the *O.T.* These "social inspectors" would be responsible for accommodating the French workers in the camps of the *O.T.* Their task would be to act as counsellors and liaison agents between the worker and the contractors in every aspect of social matters and the material conditions of the life of the workers. They were recruited from among the unfit soldiers of the Legion of French Volunteers against Bolshevism, some after serious wounds, others after the troubles caused by the cold winter of 1941-42. These former legionnaires, trained in Brittany under the direction of *Lieutenant* Sinninger, the former security chief of the legion, received instruction related to social affairs. Each promotion of social inspectors bore the name of a symbol of this legion: "*Promotion of 1st December*" in memory of the

The abandoned twin turret of Karola *in 1945 (coll. SHM).*

attack at Djukowo, the first action of the French in the East. ; "*Promotion Lieutenant Dupont*", in memory of the first officer killed... While the majority of the workers were French, the *O.T.* also recruited from every quarter – North-Africans, Italians, Belgians, Dutch, Spanish, Portuguese, Polish, Czech, Hungarian and even Indo-Chinese... The percentage of workers from the French North-African colonies was around 10%: the most numerous were Africans arriving in France just before the war; there were also some Moroccans arriving at the end of mid-1942. The North-Africans were, however, only in a state of semi-liberty. They were effectively under guard from the work site exit to the train which transported them to their camp.

If the ports of Brest, Lorient and Saint-Nazaire were already defended by guns with a calibre in excess of 20 cm, it was planned to put in place new batteries to protect several other important ports: Le Havre (Bléville, 38 cm battery), Guernsey for the protection of the west coast of the Cotentin (Battery *Mirus*, 30.5cm), Ile de Groix for the strengthening of Lorient (20.3 cm battery), La Rochelle (Ile de Ré, 20.3 cm battery), Bordeaux (La Coubre-Royan, 24 cm battery). With the exception of Le Havre, these batteries would all be operational two years later... On 29th September 1942, a conference took place in Germany between Hitler, Göring, Speer and von Rundstedt, with the generals of engineers, Jakob and Schmetzer. The question concerned the works of defence in the west which were to be completed by 1st May 1943; the *Organisation Todt* was ordered to construct 15,000 concrete bunkers which would shelter 300,000 troops permanently.

Following the Allied landing in North Africa on 9th November 1942, the German army occupied the whole of France; the *Organisation Todt* was now charged with protecting the Mediterranean coasts against a landing. The guns, materials and work force necessary for the construction of the "*Südwall*" were going to be considerably augmented... On 16th February 1943, the French state proclaimed the law establishing the obligatory work service (*S.T.O.*). Every young Frenchman born between 1st January 1920 and 31st December 1922 must enrol for two years' work in German factories. It was very difficult to escape this forced labour, in the sense that those who were affected by this measure must register at the town hall before 27th February 1943, or otherwise risk imprisonment from three months to five years and a fine of two hundred to one hundred thousand francs. Numerous young Frenchmen required for the *S.T.O.* preferred to work in France on the Atlantic Wall, rather than leave for Germany. A certain number of them were also engaged in espionage. In May 1943, a total of 291,000 persons of more than twenty different nationalities worked for the *O.T.* in France! The preceding month, the record for concrete poured had been attained with 800,000 cubic metres...

After having reached their maximum in April 1943, the number of *O.T.* personnel would begin to decline thereafter. During the summer of 1943, 50,000 French labourers who worked on the Atlantic Wall in France were sent to repair the Ruhr dams destroyed by Allied aircraft. As the war reached a turning point and the *BBC* radio broadcasts repeatedly stated that those who worked for the Germans would be punished after the Liberation...the number of absentees would accelerate. The works on the fortifications, principally the supply of materials, were also considerably slowed down by Allied air forces which gained almost total aerial supremacy.

At the end of year 1943, the western command of the *O.T.* circulated the following statement to French personnel who worked for them: "*We take this opportunity to thank the French workers in the* O.T. *for the efficient help that they have given us this year. We, the Germans, are thrown into this war, not because we wished it, but because it was forced upon us. We have, before the conflict and the precarious state that you are well aware of, built a new state and a new life. We have created a socialism that exists in no other part of the world. Our personnel are insured against illness and accidents at work, for those who work for us and their work is highly valued. This is the socialism we defend. We proclaim this for all workers, for we know that even in wartime in the capitalist countries, it is considered just as an objective for earning money. It is against this state of affairs that we fight so fanatically on your behalf. We have extended a hand to you. We seek to construct a new Europe with you. French worker, think of your children's welfare. Do you sincerely believe that they would be happier under the Anglo-American capitalist regime or bloody communism? No. It is to insure their future that we seek to institute the socialist regime in Europe. It will triumph or perish in sad chaos. It will succeed because its workers wish to live.*"

The proclamation and the various entitlements (for separation, bombardment, dangerous work) had little effect, the numbers of *O.T.* personnel not ceasing to decline. Nevertheless, a worker employed by the *O.T.* earned on average 3,000 francs a month in 1943, which was well above the average offered elsewhere. As a consequence, the recourse to forced labour accelerated. Former prisoners-of-war, as well as Polish and Russian civilians, were grouped together in camps in the north of France and supervised by armed soldiers. These forced labourers earned only a meagre wage and had very little or no freedom of movement. From the end of 1943, many of them would take part in the setting up of the secret bases for the German *V1* and *V2* rockets; these launch sites were located in areas facing England. A second defensive line was thus emerging behind the coastal fortifications.

While the members of the *O.T.* were not at risk in pre-war Germany, during it they found themselves in dangerous situations in the occupied regions, sometimes close to the front line. Increasingly, as they came to rely more and more on forced labour, it was necessary to provide supervision. One German member of the *O.T.* for every ten, where possible, was armed with a pistol or rifle generally

A twin 20.3 cm gun turret of Battery Karola *installed on the Ile de Ré to protect access to the port of* La Rochelle *(coll. AC).*

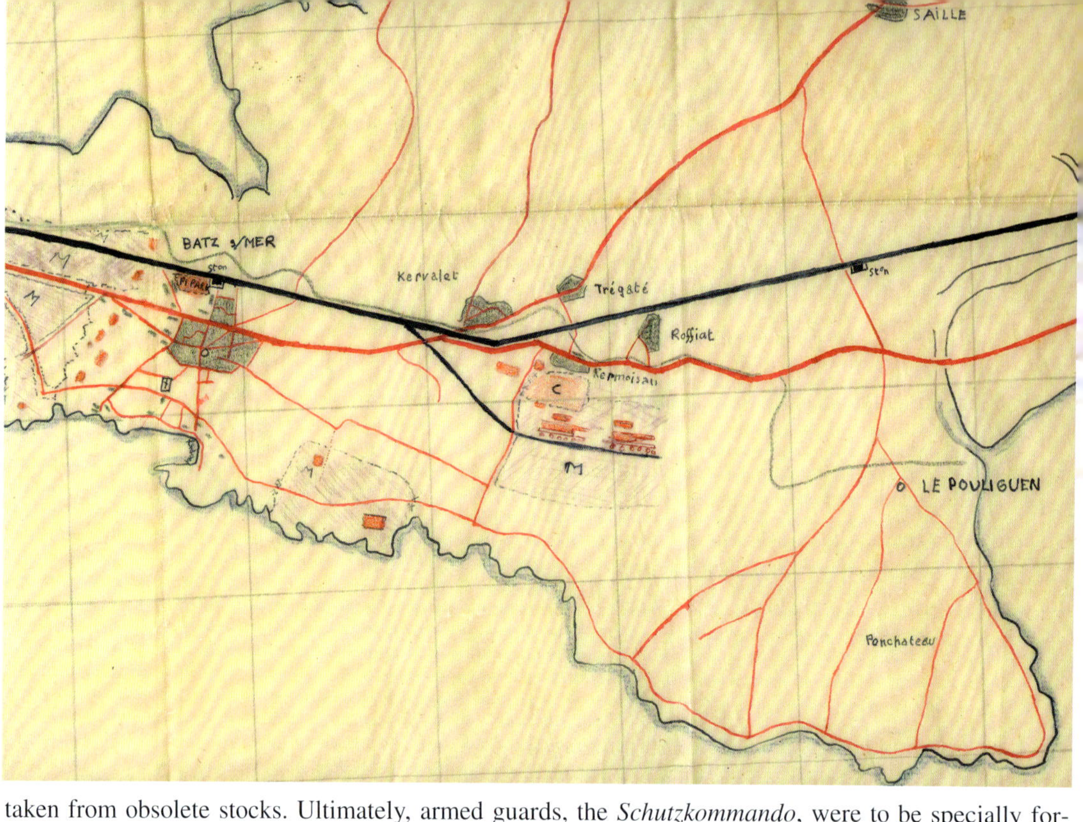

A plan of the battery at Batz-sur-Mer with its two railway guns, drawn on tracing paper by a member of the French underground network, which was transmitted to London.

taken from obsolete stocks. Ultimately, armed guards, the *Schutzkommando*, were to be specially formed to protect the work sites and the inhabitants; theoretically, one soldier would supervise 20 workers.

In Brittany, a training establishment for the *Schutzkommando* directed by *Oberstabs-frontführer* Braun was opened for Germans as well as Belgians, Dutch, Ukrainians and French. Until 9th April 1943, the courses, given by members of units of the German police, were held in the grounds of the girls high school at Pontivy. Subsequently, these personnel were trained near Paris in Camp Beauregard at La Celle Saint-Cloud. The trainees were also sent to follow a series of courses to become NCOs in the *O.T.* at the school at the Château de Pont-Callec, north of Lorient, directed by *Oberführer* Schwer. These NCOs trained at Ponr-Callec in their turn ensured the training of the future *Schutzkommando*.

Fire-direction post of the naval battery of Bégot at Plouharnel on the Quiberon peninsula (coll. SHM).

At the beginning of 1944, the extension of the *S.T.O.* to all Frenchmen born up to 31st December 1924, was above all instrumental in provoking the entry of very many young men into the Maquis. On 15th April 1944, the *O.T.* created its own information office, the Schutzkorps. This corps of some 800 civilians, subordinated to the *S.D.* (*Sicherheitsdienst*), was attached to the various field commands in France. Notably, these men accompanied the gendarmes in their search for forced labour. In vain, the Germans extended the means of control and repression in an attempt to check the escape of their personnel. They also endeavoured to combat the networks of French intelligence which rapidly spread to inform the British on the movement of German troops in France and of their military installations, principally those of the Atlantic Wall. These networks were linked either to *France-Libre* (*B.C.R.A.* in London and Algeria) or to the British special services (S.O.E.) or the Americans (O.S.S.). Combined with the low altitude reconnaissance of the Royal Air Force, this information collected directly on French soil permitted the Allies to gain an excellent knowledge of the German disposition.

A naval casemate for a 17 cm gun at Fort de l'Eve, camouflaged as a villa. A metal rod above the embrasure allows the curtain to be drawn ! *(coll. SHM).*

An anti-tank wall, 2 metres high and 2 metres thick was constructed in front of the seaside villas at La Baule. The trompe-l'œil paintings, seen from the sea, are intended to represent windows and rows of shrubs.

The fire-direction post of the 24 cm battery at Batz-sur-Mer camouflaged as a villa, in the St-Nazaire sector.

North Africans in the uniform of the Organisation Todt *at Cherbourg in March 1944 during a reunion intended to encourage their compatriots to rejoin this unit ; on the left, Mohamed El Maadi, founder of the Committee Musulman of North Africa, chief editor of the journal,* "El-Rachid", *nicknamed* "SS-Mohamed".

The school for girls at Pontivy houses the headquarters of the OT Schutzkommandos.

French musicians of the OT Schutzkommandos *prepare for a march past in Paris on November 9th, 1943.*

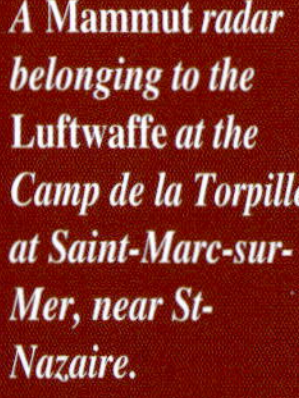

A Mammut *radar belonging to the* Luftwaffe *at the Camp de la Torpille at Saint-Marc-sur-Mer, near St-Nazaire.*

A Würzburg Riese *radar in Normandy.*

Fire-direction post of the Battery Kora-Karola *on the Ile de Ré ; unusually, it serves both the army and navy.*

Newspaper propaganda photograph : the anti-tank wall at Soulac-sur-Mer in Fortress Gironde South which, with Fortress Royan to the north, blocks the access to the port of Bordeaux.

In the fortress of Le Havre, French journalists are conducted on a visit to the construction of the formwork for an R644 *casemate, destined to receive an armoured machine gun cupola.*

Guns of the battery at Chiberta in Les Landes (coll. AC).

Casemate and fire-direction post of Battery Barbara *near Biarritz, in south-west France* (coll. AC).

Timber formwork to the interior sections of a bunker (coll. ECPAD).

8.8 cm gun at the Point de Rochebonne, in the St-Malo sector (coll. BA).

Exterior timber formwork to a casemate at Ozouville in Normandy (coll. NA).

Young Frenchmen, conscripted into the compulsory labour service (STO), unload cement trucks at the station in St-André-des-Eaux, in the St-Nazaire sector.

A little train used by the Organisation Todt *to convey building materials for the bunkers at Pouliguen in the St-Nazaire sector.*

Italian workers are used to frame this casemate with an armoured cupola at Guérande in the St-Nazaire sector.

Casemate for a 15 cm gun at La Couarde on the Ile de Ré (coll. SHM).

*Camouflaged type **R652** casemate of the battery at Chaume in Vendée protecting a French 10.5 cm gun recovered during the campaign in France* (coll. BA).

Map of the Fortresses of the Atlantic Wall.

Liberation of the Fortresses

Dunkerque : May 8th 1945
Calais : September 30th 1944
Cap Gris Nez : September 29th 1944
Boulogne : September 22th 1944
Le Havre : September 12th 1944
Cherbourg : June 26th 1944
Channel Islands : May 8th 1945
Saint-Malo : September 2nd 1944
Brest : September 19th 1944
Lorient : May 10th 1945
Saint-Nazaire : May 11st 1945
La Rochelle : May 8th 1945
Royan : April 18th 1945
Pointe de Grave : April 20th 1945

Dunkerque
Cap Gris Nez
Calais
Boulogne
Cherbourg
Le Havre
îles Anglo-Normandes
Paris
St-Malo
Brest
Lorient
St-Nazaire
OCEAN ATLANTIQUE
La Rochelle
Royan
Pointe de Grave
MER MEDITERRANEE

A Tobruk pit for a machine gun in Brittany (coll. AC).

Field-Marshal Rommel takes command of the Atlantic Wall

At the end of the year 1943, the German high command knew that an Allied invasion was only a question of months. The outcome of the war would be played out on the Atlantic Wall, but it presented numerous weaknesses between the major ports. Directive No.51 of 3rd November 1943 detailed the precise measures to make these good: *The hard and costly fight against Bolshevism which has lasted for two and a half years, has subjected our entire military forces to the greatest trials. This reflects the increasing danger and general situation. The latter has since changed. The danger from the east remains, but another greater still arises in the west: the Anglo-Saxon invasion. In the east, the extent of the territory permits us, in unfavourable conditions, to lose important ground without fatal consequences for the vital sinews of Germany. It will be different in the west. If the enemy succeeds in making a large breach in our defensive front, the immediate consequences will be unpredictable. All the indications show that the enemy will move to the offensive against the western front, at the latest in the coming spring, perhaps even sooner. As a consequence, I cannot take responsibility any longer for weakening the western front for the benefit of other operational theatres. I have resolved therefore to reinforce the defensive capacity there, in particular where we can begin long-range operations against England. For it is from there that the enemy will launch his attack and there, if we are not misled, that the decisive battle will be fought. Holding and diversionary attacks on other fronts must be expected. A large-scale attack on Denmark is not ruled out. It would be more difficult to sustain by sea, and less effective by air. But the political and operational consequences would be considerable if it succeeds. At the outset of the battle, the entire offensive force of the enemy will be forcibly directed against the troops occupying the coast. Only by intensifying the construction of defences, which should be pushed to the maximum by committing all the material and personnel resources of the* Reich *and the occupied territories, can we consolidate our coastal defences in the available time, which actually appears quite short. The fixed armament (anti-tank guns, buried tanks, coast artillery, landward defence weapons, mines, etc.) which will shortly reach Denmark and the western occupied territories, will be concentrated directly in the principal points of impact on the most vulnerable coastal sectors. If, nevertheless, the enemy succeeds after landing in concentrating all his forces, it will find itself opposed by a counter-attack capable of containing the development of a landing and throwing the enemy back into the sea. In conclusion, one must be able, by emergency measures prepared in the smallest detail and withdrawing as rapidly as possible from the less threatened sectors of the coast and the* Reich, *to throw everything into the battle against the enemy landing. The air force and navy must be capable, with all available forces, of engaging the enemy without reserve in the most powerful aerial and naval assault which they are capable of. Instructions were similarly given to armoured units of the army that they should be held close to the coast in order to intervene in the event of attack. The available Flak units must be equally brought forward and new field aerodromes constructed. As for the navy, new heavy calibre coast batteries should be installed as quickly as possible and the submarines held ready to intercept an invasion fleet. On Rommel's direct recommendation after his inspection of December 1943, a naval battery of 21 cm Skoda guns would be placed at Crisbecq in Normandy. That would particularly displease the Allies, for it was the only gun exceeding 15.5 cm calibre to be found in the future invasion sector!*

As proof of the strategic importance given to the Atlantic Wall, on 5th November 1943, the celebrated and popular *Field-Marshal* Rommel was appointed Inspector of the Atlantic Wall. In January 1944, he also received the command of Army Group B, extending from the north of Holland to Saint-Nazaire, the eventual invasion zone. As a consequence of his inspections, Rommel perceived only too well the weaknesses which characterised this line of fortifications: In the first place, the soldiers who were stationed on the Atlantic Wall were not elite troops. The battle-hardened troops were progressively withdrawn from this sector to be engaged on the eastern front where the German army would count 80% of its losses. Those who remained were less fit, often older or very young. Amongst them were to be found Russians, Georgians, Poles, Czechs who were often forcibly conscripted into the German army. Marshal Rommel would, however, try to raise their morale. When he was satisfied with the efficiency and camouflage of a battery, he gave an accordion to its crew! The armament of the Atlantic Wall was also is disparate as the troops who guarded it, the best equipment having been sent to the east. It relied principally on the confiscated stocks from the arsenals of the countries which the Germans had invaded in the first years of the war: the artillery machine guns were often Czech, Polish, Belgian, Dutch, French…with ammunition supplies which did not always allow their crews to exercise. Training shoots against sea targets were particularly rare! Other equipment came from 1914-18 war stocks, disarmed warships, obsolete tanks. Only the Pas-de-Calais sector mounted truly modern, powerful and effective guns to face an Allied armada.

Placing undetectable wooden mines on the Atlantic Wall in February 1944.

Field Marshal *Erwin Rommel, "father" of the Atlantic Wall. He would be forced to commit suicide after being implicated in the failed assassination attempt against Hitler of July 20th, 1944 (coll. AC).

German propaganda did not cease to send journalists to this part of the "Wall", to convince the entire world that it was as powerful as its entire length... If the large ports were well defended, the remainder of the Atlantic Wall did not represent an homogeneous and continuous defensive line.

To oblige the Allied troops to land in an exposed area and to hinder the movement of their armour, Rommel proposed to place more than 50,000 obstacles on the beaches. Tetrahedra in steel or wood, usually surmounted by a mine, were able to penetrate the landing craft if they arrived at high tide, as well as posts embedded in the sand which were given the name of "*Rommel's Asparagus*". Defensive obstacles previously used by the countries invaded by Germany were reused; Czech hedgehogs, Belgian gates and even obstacles from the Maginot Line! They allowed the German artillery to engage the Allied tanks which would be halted or slowed down. Planted in the fields, the "asparagus" would prevent aircraft and gliders from landing. Further, to counter enemy parachute landings, the hinterland was flooded. Finally, numerous networks of barbed wire would hamper the progress of the enemy infantry, as well as tens of thousands of mines, including naval mines sown at sea. On his orders, several naval coastal batteries were emplaced on the parts of the coast lying between the ports which did not possess long-range artillery. In five months, Marshal Rommel gave a new face to the Atlantic Wall which was much more dangerous. But much work was still under way in the spring of 1944, particularly the construction of powerful batteries at Le Havre and in Guernsey for the defence of the port of Cherbourg. Along 6,000 kilometres of coastline, the army disposed around 4,000 guns from 3.7 cm to 28 cm, the navy 1,500 guns up to 40.6 cm calibre, while anti- aircraft defences numbered some 1,400 guns from 2 cm to 12.8 cm.

While the great majority of the German forces were permanently stationed on the Atlantic Wall defences and principally in the ports, their reserve forces were placed in the country to the rear in order to intervene directly there or wherever danger arose. Among these reserve troops were the redoubtable panzer divisions...But Rommel did not have the authority for their movement. Persuaded that the battle would be decided within the first 24 hours, he favoured the protection of the entire coastal zone in order to throw the attacking force back into the sea. But he alone could not make that decision and had to defer to the conceptions of *Marshal* von Rundstedt, the supreme military commander in the west, who preferred to conduct a decisive counter-attack inland.

On the left, translator Wilhelm Makus, accompanied by four recruits from the East serving in the Marine Flak *in the Saint-Nazaire sector.*

Recreated hospital at Raversijde.

Concrete tetrahedra surmounted by a stake on the beach at Pouliguen.

MG34 *machine gun on a heavy stand in a casemate* (coll. AC).

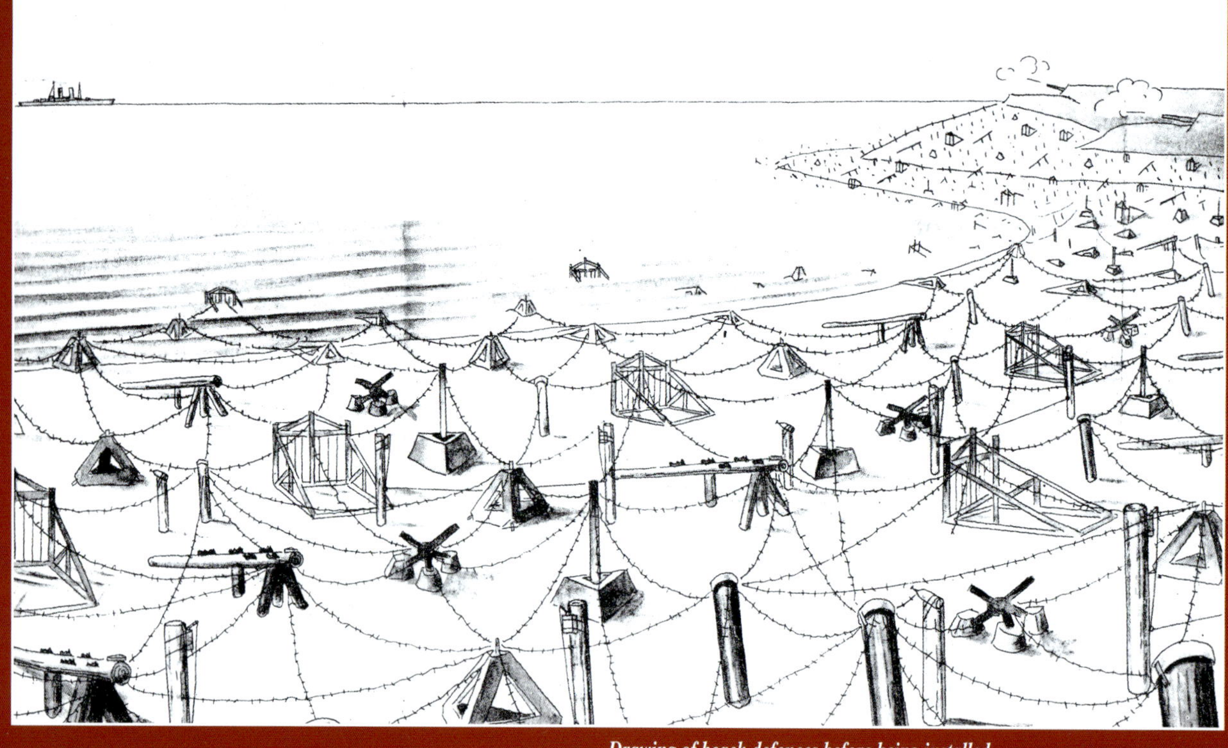

Drawing of beach defences before being installed, prepared by Field Marshal *Rommel* (coll. AC).

An officer of the army artillery – Le Grand Blockhaus.

Italian artillery captain – certain Italian units held positions on the Atlantic Wall – Le Grand Blockhaus.

Inspection of troops at Le Havre by Field Marshal *Rommel at the beginning of 1944* (coll. AC).

Beach defences in front of the town of Le Havre (coll. AC).

Inspection by Field Marshal *Rommel of the Battery des Arros at Soulac in 1944* (coll. BA).

Cossack officer from Kouban enrolled into the German army – Le Grand Blockhaus.

A casemate of the Crisbecq Battery armed with a Czech 24 cm Skoda *gun, the most powerful in the entire invasion zone* *(coll. NA).*

The Atlantic Wall faces the invasion

The Allies had fixed the place and date of the invasion at the time of the Quebec conference in August 1943: it would take place in France on the beaches of Normandy in first days of the month of May 1944. General Eisenhower, the commander-in-chief of the Allied forces, pushed back the date one month to engage more important forces in a larger sector than that seen in the initial plan. The invasion, on which the outcome of the war would depend, was thus fixed for the beginning of June 1944. To prepare for this invasion, the Allies assembled then trained more than 3 million men in the south of England; 1.7 million British, 1.5 million Americans, 200,000 Canadians, Australians and New Zealanders, as well as 70,000 soldiers from other countries. Among these were found mainly Polish, Belgians, Dutch and French who had escaped from their country invaded by the German army.

The armada set up by the Allies was of the highest order: on the maritime level, 5,000 warships and 1,600 merchant ships were assembled. In order to prevent the German submarines, the U-boats, from intervening from their bases on the French coast, the ships of the Royal Navy laid thousands of sea mines in the approaches to the Channel. The aerial supremacy of the Allies was totally overwhelming in the face of a *Luftwaffe* which was only a shadow of its former self. The Allies assembled some 16,000 machines of which 3,500 were gliders. Besides, General Eisenhower promised his troops: "*If you see aircraft in the sky on D-Day, don't worry, they are ours.*" To neutralise the German defences to the maximum, the aircraft of the Royal Air Force and the U.S. Army Air Force would fly over 200,000 sorties in the north-west quarter of France during the ten weeks preceding the invasion! To confuse the Germans, two missions were carried out in the Pas-de-Calais for every one in Normandy. A phantom army was also assembled in the north of England to create the impression that the principal attack would take place in northern France…

If the means for transporting and protecting the Allied troops in Normandy were to succeed, the crucial problem lay in the lack of a port. How could the hundreds of tons of heavy materiel, as well as the supply of the tens of thousands of troops on the ground be landed? In fact, if a landing seemed to have a good chance of success on the beaches of Normandy, it was out of the question for the Allies to take simultaneously one, or several, ports which had been transformed into impregnable fortresses by the Germans: Cherbourg to the west or Le Havre to the east. It was Winston Churchill who found the solution to the German strategy: they did not care to attack frontally one of these large impregnable ports – they would construct their own. In the greatest secrecy, they constructed the prefabricated elements of artificial ports in England. This was the "*Mulberry*" project. Dozens of enormous concrete caissons called Phoenix would be towed across the Channel and then sunk in accordance with a precise plan for two ports in front of the Normandy beaches. Obsolete vessels would be sunk to act as breakwaters. The first port, "*Mulberry A*", would be constructed in the American sector before St-Laurent-sur-Mer, the second, christened "*Port Winston*", before Arromanches in the British sector. The landing would be carried out at dawn on the beaches at mid-tide. Those where the Americans would land would be codenamed *Utah* and *Omaha*, the beaches of *Gold* and *Sword* would be the objectives of the British troops, while that of the Canadians was called *Juno*. On 5th June shortly after 16.00 hours, General Eisenhower gave the order for the launch of Operation OVERLORD. The assault would take place on the morning of 6th June. As the weather was very bad, Marshal Rommel obtained permission during the day of the fifth to leave for Germany, notably to present some shoes to his wife...In fact, he wished above all to obtain Hitler's authorisation to bring forward the armoured divisions to the coast.

Oberleutnant MA, *Walter Ohmsen, commander of the Crisbecq Battery, was awarded the Knight's Cross ; his battery sank an American destroyer and resisted several American ground attacks (coll. BA).*

The French Resistance had been alerted by radio of the imminent attack: the reading of the verses by Verlaine, "*Les sanglots longs des violons de l'automne*", gave the signal for the disruption of the German means of communication; the Resistance would blow up bridges and railway tracks to prevent German reinforcements from reaching the invasion zone. To take control of the bridges and the German communication routes behind the beaches, a little after midnight, the Allies despatched their elite forces, the parachutists. Two American divisions, the 82nd and 101st, each comprising 7,500 men, were transported in 822 *C47* aircraft and dropped behind *Utah* Beach. Dummy parachutists in the form of dolls dressed as American soldiers, armed with small explosive charges that exploded on impact with the ground, served to disorientate the enemy. The real American parachutists were, for their part, armed with a small metal cricket as a sign of recognition for the purpose of assembling the combat groups. Ste-Marie-du-Mont and Ste-Mère-l'Eglise would be the first villages liberated in their sector. The 12,000 British parachutists of the 6th Airborne Division, known as "*The Red Devils*", landed behind *Sword* Beach where many gliders were lost with their contents on landing. Major Howard's unit took the bridges at Bénouville and Ranville to the sound of the bagpipes.

At dawn, 2,210 Allied aircraft carried out a final bombardment of the German positions which would soon be taken by assault. The Germans, whose radar installations had been confused, only knew that they were under attack at the moment they observed the silhouettes of the thousands of ships that appeared on the horizon! Soon after, at 05.45 hours, the hell was renewed on the German fortifications which were targeted by the long-range guns of the warships. During this time, the landing craft charged towards the beaches which would be reached at 06.30 hours; some of these were equipped with multiple rocket-launchers. Allied air superiority was such that only two German fighters would arrive to fly over the landing zones during the day of 6th June! Once disembarked on the beaches, the Allied assault troops rushed on towards the German positions which were taken one after the other. Amphibious tanks or those fitted to explode mines, christened "*Funnies*", for breaching the obstacles or placing perforated tracks on the sand, had been invented for the occasion. However, the losses were

losses were heavy, especially at *Omaha* where the preparatory bombardment had failed; the beach would be renamed "*Bloody Omaha*". Soldiers of the American 2nd Ranger Battalion, commanded by Lieutenant-Colonel Rudder, scaled the cliffs to gain access to the German battery at Pointe du Hoc; they were extremely surprised to find guns there...made of wood! On Rommel's orders, the guns had been withdrawn to the rear to escape destruction from the air. The French also participated in this historic day: at sea in the vessels of the Free French naval forces, as well as on land where the 177 Naval Fusiliers of Commando Kieffer led the assault on the strongpoint in the casino at Ouistreham at the cost of losses representing half of the force. Above all, the Americans, the British and the Canadians were to set foot on French soil. By the evening of 6th June, 156,000 men had been landed with 20,000 vehicles of all types. The Atlantic Wall had not prevented the invasion, the Allied losses in terms of ships were minimal. Overlord, the greatest invasion operation of all time, had succeed. It had cost the Allies around 10,000 dead, wounded or missing.

General de Gaulle, who had embodied the hope of innumerable French people during the occupation, landed in his turn on the soil of Normandy. He, who had launched an appeal to the Resistance on 18th June 1940, was now head of the provisional government of the French Republic. Throughout his journey, the civilians came out in their hundreds to acclaim him with cries of "*Vive de Gaulle*". He would commit himself to restoring the authority of the Republic.

This second lieutenant of signals wished to communicate news of the invasion in this casemate, but the line had been cut by the French Resistance – Mémorial de Quinéville.

A concrete anti-tank wall with a firing position for an MG34 machine gun extending from a casemate for a 5 cm anti-tank gun in the Quinéville sector.

An armoured cupola for an MG34 machine gun after the fighting at Les Gougins, to the north of Utah Beach (coll. NA).

These members of the Organisation Todt from the Cherbourg sector wait to be transferred to a prison camp in England (coll. NA).

A camouflaged casemate of the naval Battery Hamburg located at Fermanville near Cherbourg, with its 24 cm gun (coll. NA).

A casemate at Ozouville in the Cherbourg sector, showing the process of assembling the steel reinforcement (coll. NA).

Rear of a camouflaged casemate at Azeville (coll. AC).

An American signals post set up in front of a casemate on **Omaha Beach** *(coll. NA).*

Americans inspect the gun in a casemate covering **Omaha** *Beach, nicknamed* **“Bloody Omaha”** *(coll. NA).*

American troops pose in front of a casemate at Pointe du Hoc, where the guns anticipated on June 6th, 1944, were not found ! (coll. NA).

Allied troops inspect one of the 15 cm guns of the battery at Longues-sur-Mer which has been damaged ; the others, still in place today, are a great tourist attraction (coll. NA).

This German soldier has been buried following an explosion in a casemate at Quinéville on June 9th, 1944 (coll. NA).

The British have installed an anti-aircraft position on the roof of a casemate at Courseulles-sur-Mer (coll. NA).

h soldiers discover a 5 cm gun in an emplacement found at Douvres, close ıajor radar station which today has been transformed into a museum.

mericans have taken up a position on a fire-direction post on the overlooking the port of Le Havre after the Liberation (coll. NA).

The fire-direction post of the battery at Riva-Bella, today transformed into a museum called "Le Grand Bunker" (coll. AC).

These German soldiers seem visibly relieved to have survived the hard combat in taking the port of Cherbourg which ended on June 25th, 1944 (coll. NA).

The difficult conquest of the ports

The Allies, who had landed over 80 kilometres of beaches, could now move on the second stage of their plan: to capture a deep-water port to secure the supply of the troops ashore. That port was Cherbourg. While the town of Montebourg was being liberated, an enormous storm unfolded at sea. It would last three days and destroy the American artificial port before *Omaha* Beach and damage the British port before Arromanches. The supply of the troops ashore was considerably reduced and the taking of the port of Cherbourg became extremely urgent. This battle commenced on 20th June 1944. The German high command, aware of the great strategic interest in this port, had decided to systematically destroy its installations: the Germans withdrew to prepare to engage in their last combat to leave time for the engineers to sink vessels to block the basins, to blow up the cranes and the quays, as well as the railways which served the port. The principal German artillery was orientated towards the sea and was thus ineffective for defence against the interior. On 23rd June, General von Schlieben, who had no illusion about the outcome of the battle, gave the order to his men to "*fight to the death*". The following day, American fighter-bombers bombarded the ground before the advance into the suburbs of the port. On 25th June, the American offensive continued and the German wounded crammed together by the hundreds in the underground headquarters of General von Schlieben. At 14.00 hours, he surrendered to the American troops. Some days later, after a ceremony in the presence of French civilians, the American General Collins came to present a gift to Doctor Renault, the mayor of Cherbourg. It was a French flag made from the fabric of an American parachute. This symbolic gesture marked the return of the town to the French civil authorities by the American army. The taking of the port of Cherbourg, which would be put back into a working state within a month, was a decisive step in the Allied victory.

On 13th June 1944, the first German *V-1* rocket had been launched against England. This new weapon, however, would not change the course of history as had been repeated regularly in German propaganda... The first *V-2* rocket would be fired on 8th September.

The taking of the port of Cherbourg was not sufficient for the Allies, for whom it was necessary to capture others to definitely ensure the supply of the invasion force. But these ports had been endowed with a ring of almost impregnable bunkers. The Americans, having arrived before the fortresses of St-Malo and Brest at the beginning of August 1944, attacked them with the greatest material means: tanks, artillery, aircraft and even with the strength of the navy. In the siege of St-Malo lasting until 2nd September, it was necessary to use napalm to bring and end to the minute fortified island of Cézembre, which had held out for the 27 days of the siege! That at Brest last for a month and a half, during which almost 10,000 GIs were killed or wounded. The port, entirely destroyed by the Germans before their surrender, was almost unusable.

This young German of the RAD, taken prisoner in the Cherbourg sector, appears strongly affected by the events (coll. NA).

The Americans have recovered the German fast patrol boat base in Cherbourg. Setting out from this base on April 27th, 1944, several Schnellboote *had carried out a raid in Lime Bay on the south coast of England where American troops were training for the invasion in* LST *landing ships – 638 men were killed there* (coll. NA).

The Cité d'Aleth at St-Malo, benefiting from a gigantic underground complex, is taken after an assault by American troops on August 17th, 1944, and conquered (coll. NA).

This German naval arti man lost his life during fighting for the fortress Brest on September 4th,

A machine gun cupola at the Cité d'Aleth in the St-Malo sector, heavily damaged in the fighting (coll. NA).

Naval **Oberleutnant** *Richard Seuss, commander on the Ile de Cézembre facing St-Malo, was decorated with the Knight's Cross on August 15th, 1944 ; for having held out against American forces until September 2nd, he would add the Oak Leaves to this decoration* (coll. NA).

The submarine base at Brest was recovered on September 19th, 1944, after a siege lasting a month and a half which cost the Americans some 10,000 killed and wounded.

Zur frommen Erinerung im Gebete an

Johann Hochstetter

in Lambertsneukirchen

Marineartillerie-Obergefreiter

geboren am 3. Oktober 1908

gefallen am 4. September 1944

in der Festung Brest

R. I. P.

Er sieht so tröstend auf uns hernieder.
Dort über den Sternen, da sehen wir uns ja wieder,
Meine Lieben und meine Kindelein,
Jetzt kehr' ich zu Euch nicht mehr heim,
Der letzte Gedanke, der letzte Blick,
Ging nochmals in die Heimat zurück.

A fire-control radar for a German naval anti-aircraft battery around Brest ; the interior has been camouflaged with a painted tree (coll. NA).

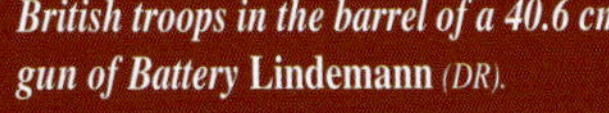

British troops in the barrel of a 40.6 cm gun of Battery Lindemann *(DR).*

Battery Todt *has been "liberated" by Canadian troops (DR).*

A Canadian soldier in front of a casemate of Battery Todt *(DR).*

This naval artillery-man grows tomatoes beside his barrack in the Saint-Nazaire Pocket.

The last fortresses of the Atlantic Wall

At the same time as the British and Canadians were liberating the ports of Le Havre, Dieppe and above all, Antwerp, which were much closer to England, the Americans did not care to repeat the very costly operation at Brest with the ports lying further south and which were still occupied by the German army. They decided to direct their principal effort towards the east.

The "Atlantic Pockets" were born. The fortresses of Dunkirk, Lorient (with Belle-Ile-en- Mer and the Ile de Groix), Saint-Nazaire, La Rochelle (with the Ile de Ré and the Ile d'Oléron), Royan and the Pointe de Grave, as well as the Channel Islands, remained in the hands of around 100,000 entrenched German soldiers. The French civilians who were trapped there were going to have to wait nine months before gaining their freedom. They would have to live under very difficult conditions, for no outside supplies could be delivered. There was no electricity or coal in what would be a very cold winter. The perimeters of the Atlantic Pockets were held by the forces of the *F.F.I.* (*Forces Françaises de l'Interieur*), the irregulars (*Francs-Tireurs*) and partisans, supported by the American army north of the Loire.

The German troops who were encircled there, however, did not remain inactive. At Saint-Nazaire, which was the largest and where 28,000 soldiers were entrenched, two attacks would be carried out to gain 120 square kilometres of cultivable land on 15th October and then, on 21st December 1944, the latter date coinciding with the last German offensive in the Ardennes. At the beginning of 1945, the commander of the Channel Islands, which still remained in the hands of German forces, decided to mount naval raids on the liberated Cotentin. The first raid was carried out against the coaling port of Granville on the night of 8th/9th March 1945, while on the other side of France the Allies were crossing the Rhine! After an artillery bombardment with 2 cm guns, three German vessels carrying 150 soldiers divided into sections penetrated the port. The landing force blew up four British coasters as well as the

cranes, and took back with them 67 German prisoners who had been taken by the Allies. A diversionary raid had also been mounted on a beach further to the north by four other vessels. Some troops had landed and taken prisoner several American officers who were staying in two hotels! A second raid would be a total failure: it entailed the port of Cherbourg, which would be subjected simultaneously to a sabotage attack from the rear and an attack from the sea. Some troops were landed successfully from the Channel Islands, but the discovery by the Allies of three rubber dinghies on a deserted beach revealed the purpose of the attack which was planned for 6th April 1945. The saboteurs were arrested and the naval assault was foiled.

In April 1945, General Larmenat received orders to reduce the Atlantic Pockets located south of the Loire. On 15th April, he launched the attack on Royan and the Pointe de Grave, German redoubts which blocked the access to the port of Bordeaux. Everything was completed in five days, but the attack had cost several hundred dead on the French side and the town of Royan had been levelled in the preparatory bombing by 1,200 *Flying Fortresses*...On 1st May 1945, the Ile d'Oléron was liberated in turn by a French landing operation. As Hitler committed suicide in his bunker and Berlin fell into the hands of the Soviets, the capture of the Atlantic Pockets was suspended. Without further fighting, the pockets of La Rochelle and Dunkirk were freed by the general German capitulation on 8th May. After giving time to the Germans to sweep mines on their approaches, those of Lorient and Saint-Nazaire were liberated on 10th and 11th May 1945 respectively. The Second World War was ended in France. After the reconstruction would come Europe's hour.

A post card sent by air to Germany for Christmas 1944 from the Saint-Nazaire Pocket.

Some weeks before the end of the war, these naval artillerymen, one of whom has acquired a submariner's pair of leather trousers, converse over a glass at La Baule, in the sector of the St-Nazaire Pocket.

The **Sherman M4A1 tank** *"Franche-Comté" of the French 2*[e] **Division Blindée,** *takes part in the suppression of the German position in the village of Fontbedeau in the sector of the Royan Pocket on April 16*[th]*, 1944.*

French troops in front of a casemate of the Battery des Arros at Soulac, with its 16.4 cm gun, taken by force in April 1945 (coll. AC).

Ceremony of the surrender of the Saint-Nazaire Pocket on May 11th, 1945 – Le Grand Blockhaus.

On May 11th, 1945, officers of the French and American navies have the functions of the submarine base at Saint-Nazaire explained to them by German submariners.

French soldiers discover the fire-direction post at Batz-sur-Mer : a Fusilier-Marin *and parachutist of the SAS – Le Grand Blockhaus.*

A French soldier from the Resistance discovers the machine gun defending the entrance to Le Grand Blockhaus.

In search of souvenirs…an era has passed, a belt buckle is exchanged for a packet of cigarettes !

This American captain looks through the entrance defence loophole…

Summer 1945, General de Larminat, former commander of the Detachment of French Forces of the Atlantic, visits the first "museum" of the Second World War installed in the town hall of La Rochelle, the Pocket having just been liberated – a mock casemate has been recreated !

Review

The Atlantic Wall was not a continuous line of impregnable works as German propaganda would wish to have us believe. In putting the accent on the most powerful installations in the Pas-de-Calais where the Wall was finished, Germany wished to assure its own people of the impossibility of the opening of a second front in the west. The Allies had sought to exploit the weakness of the Atlantic Wall in landing the weaker defended beaches of Basse-Normandie.

At the Liberation, the French army had recovered hundreds of coastal batteries, often intact. Few being protected, they were rapidly dismantled then pillaged by the scrap merchants amidst general indifference. Practically all of the guns would disappear, except for the soon-to- be celebrated battery of Longues-sur-Mer in Normandy. Its casemates, with their guns forever pointed seawards – memorials of past rivalries between European countries – are now in effect taken by assault by the armies of visitors! As an integral part of our historic heritage – last vestiges of 2,000 years of French fortification – the bunkers are now important testimonies of our collective European memory. Much has disappeared and it is high time that the authorities endeavoured to preserve them, as has been achieved in Normandy with the classification of the most remarkable as historic monuments. The heritage services of other European countries, even those less fortified than France, have understood that they must protect these remains of an astonishing architecture. Many have been transformed into guardians of peace, destined to pass on their history to younger generations. There are thus very fine museums in Norway, Denmark, Holland and Belgium. The first prize for preservation goes to very British conservationists: there are more museums on the Atlantic Wall on each of the Channel Islands of Jersey and Guernsey than along the entire French coast! It is sad to note that the majority of the preserved sites on our coasts are due to the courageous initiative of a few enthusiasts! We hope that this book will contribute to a better understanding and the preservation of this relatively neglected part of our military heritage.